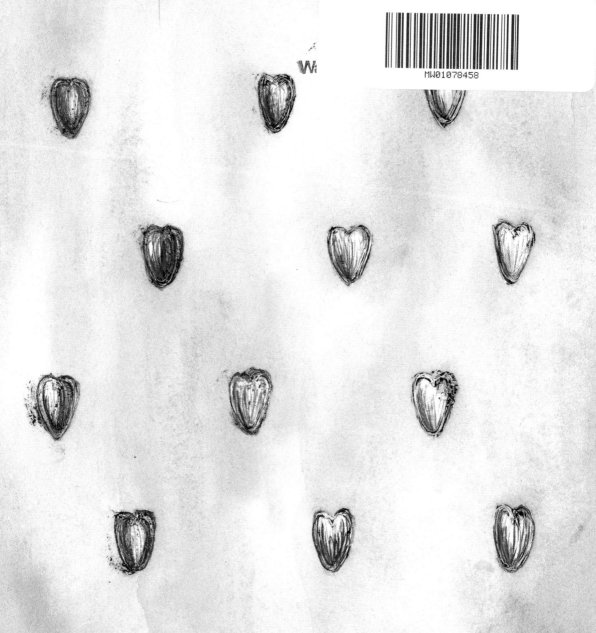

For Cleopatra M.

Viking

Published by Penguin Group

Penguin Young Readers Group, 345 Hudson Street, New York, New York 10014, U.S.A.

Penguin Books Ltd, 80 Strand, London WC2R 0RL, England

Penguin Books Australia Ltd, 250 Camberwell Road, Camberwell, Victoria 3124, Australia

Penguin Books Canada Ltd, 10 Alcorn Avenue, Toronto, Ontario, Canada M4V 3B2

Penguin Books (N.Z.) Ltd, 182-190 Wairau Road, Auckland 10, New Zealand

First published in 2004 by Viking, a division of Penguin Young Readers Group

1 3 5 7 9 10 8 6 4 2

LIBRARY OF CONGRESS CATALOGING-IN-PUBLICATION DATA

Greenstein, Elaine.

One little seed / written and illustrated by Elaine Greenstein.

p. cm.

Summary: Follows a seed from the time it is planted until it grows into a beautiful flower.

ISBN 0-670-03633-1 (Hardcover)

[1. Flowers—Fiction. 2. Growth (Plants)—Fiction.] I. Title.

PZ7.G8517Or 2004   [E]—dc22   2003019769

Manufactured in China

Set in American typewriter

Book design by Nancy Brennan

One Little Seed

By Elaine Greenstein

Viking

one little seed

dropped in a hole

watered and loved

roots unfurl

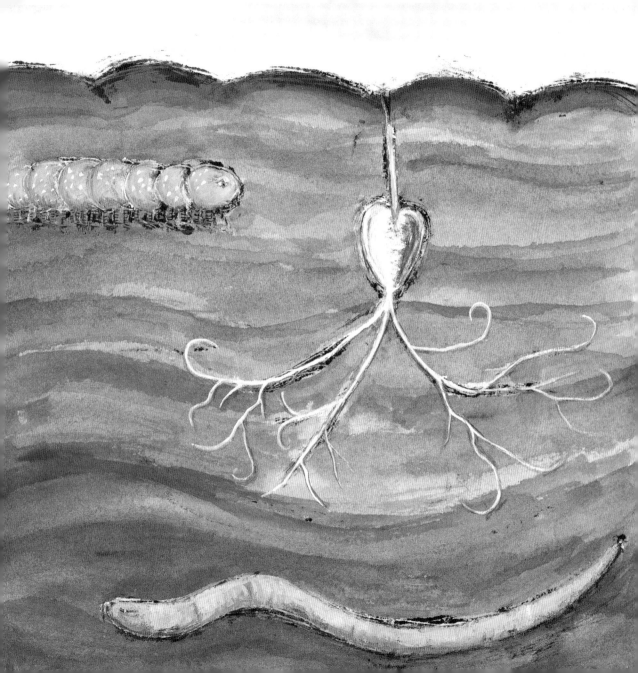

sprout uncurls

stretch in rain

weed and watch

bud bursts out

sun shines bright

blooms blossom

one little seed
is picked